On the edge of a small town in the country
lies Big Park. Big Park is a special place
where magical creatures join in games
and sports. When the boys and girls visit
Big Park they love to join in too...

Katy is a cat. She lives by the side of the old house in Big Park.

Katy is different from other cats because she only has one eye. Most of the creatures who visit Big Park will not play with her because they think she is not very good at games and sport.

Katy would watch the other
creatures play ball games and
wish that she could play too.

Fergal the fox could jump high,
but he could not throw the ball into
the net no matter how hard he tried.

Selina the hare could run fast
but she could not throw the
ball into the net either.

"Go away," said Fergal,
"you only have one eye
and can't play properly!"

"Go away" said Selina,
"you can't play.
You only have one eye and
you will lose the game!"

So Katy would play all by herself,
throwing the ball over and over again.

Then, one day, Harvey the
coach came by and watched.

Swoooosh!
Every time she threw the ball it
dropped into the net.

Harvey was flabbergasted.

"Hi Katy," called Harvey.
"Hi Harvey," called Katy.

"Why do you play all by yourself?"
asked Harvey.

"No one will play with me,"
said Katy.

"That is unfair," said Harvey,
"very unfair indeed, but I need
creatures like you for my team.
Come with me."

Harvey took Katy to
the other side of Big Park
where boys and girls
were playing a game
called basketball.

It was a fast game,
a very fast game indeed.

"Hi team," called Harvey.

"This is Katy. I know how she can help us. Our team finds it hard to score and to win games we need to score".

"Katy, with her one good eye is good at scoring. She must join our team today".

Katy could not believe her eye when she saw the looks on their faces.

The team wanted her to play!

Soon all the Big Park creatures
had heard the news.

Gabby the duck, Tyler the tortoise,
Lofty the wallaby, even Fergal and
Selina came to watch.
How surprised they all were to
see Katy playing basketball.

They could not believe their eyes
either when each time the team
passed the ball to Katy she threw
it right through the net.

Katy scored not one,

not two,

but three baskets!

Swoosh!

Swoosh!

Swoosh!

"Hat-trick!" quacked Gabby.

"What is a hat-trick?"
asked Tyler, waking up.

"I don't know," said Gabby,
"but I heard Harvey shout
'hat-trick' the other day."

"It means three scores,"
said Buster Morley, the little boy.

"We know", said Birdie Lewis, the little girl,
"because when we play football
we score hat-tricks".

All of a sudden all the creatures
loved Katy, and they shouted and cheered.
Even Fergal and Selina gave her a clap.

"We all know Katy is different,"
said Harvey,
"but she can do with one eye what
we often find difficult with two eyes."

To celebrate, the creatures put Katy
on Big Park Rock and she was awarded
a medal and the special Match Ball.

"Hurray for Katy," they all cried.
"Three cheers for Katy!"

That night as Katy lay on the roof of the old house in Big Park, she looked up at the sky and hoped that one day she would be a basketball shooting star.

Do you think she will?

Kelly's Questions...

1. What kind of animal is Katy?

2. What colour is Katy's eye patch?

3. What is a hat-trick?

4. Why were the other creatures wrong to think that Katy wasn't good at sport?

5. How did Katy feel when she wasn't allowed to play?

6. Why do you think Harvey wanted to help Katy?

7. How did Katy feel when the other animals let her join their game?

8. How did Katy feel when everyone gave her a cheer?

9. Why is it good to let other people join in games?

Meet the Big Park friends

**Katy
the cat**

**Gabby
the duck**

**Hutch
the rabbit**

**Charlie
the cockerel**

**Selina
the hare**

**Birdie
Lewis**

**Rusty
the squirrel**

**Dillon
the mouse**

**Buster
Morley**

**Chip
the monkey**

**Joey
the snail**

**Fergal
the fox**

**Polly
the pig**

**Tyler
the tortoise**

**Lofty
the wallaby**

**Harvey
the frog**

**Hazel
the squirrel**

Other titles from Big Park Books...

**Lofty Lands
the Winner**

**Gabby Goes
for Gold**

**Tyler Takes on
the Marathon**